Shopkins™

Once you shop...You can't stop!

WELCOME TO CHEF CLUB!

ADAPTED BY LEIGH STEPHENS

SCHOLASTIC INC.

ISBN 978-1-338-11807-0

10 9 8 7 6 5 4 3 2 1   17 18 19 20 21

Printed in the U.S.A.   40

First printing 2017

Book design by Erin McMahon

EARLY ONE MORNING, THE TOWN OF SHOPVILLE was quiet and still when suddenly—

Click-clack! Click-clack! Click-clack!

The sound of Bubbleisha's platform shoes echoed through the sleepy streets as she ran through Shopville. She pulled out her phone and frantically tapped at the touch screen to make a call.

"I can't wait to wake everyone up and tell them the greatest news!" she squealed. Her first call was to Cheeky Chocolate, who was fast asleep on the Sweet Treats shelf in Small Mart, her head resting on a comfy cotton candy pillow.

"Hello? Bubbleisha?" answered Cheeky drowsily. "The sun's not even warm yet . . ."

"You'll never guess what I just heard!" Bubbleisha shouted into the phone.

Cheeky whipped off her sleep mask and threw her ribbon-candy blanket aside. "Tell me! Tell me!" She leapt from her bed as she listened to Bubbleisha's news. "No way! I've got to call Sprinkles. Hold on, I'll group chat her in."

Cheeky dialed Miss Sprinkles, who decided that her friend Lippy Lips also had to hear the news. Lippy called Strawberry Tubs, who called Jessicake, who called Kooky Cookie. Soon, Apple Blossom and Donatina were on the call, too. Bubbleisha eagerly shared her news with everyone.

"There's a new Shoppie and some new Shopkins in Shopville, and they're starting a new club at the Cooking Academy!" Bubbleisha blurted out.

The Shoppies and Shopkins cheered with excitement and all began talking at once.

"What?"

"No way!"

"We have to join!"

"To the Cooking Academy!" cried Apple Blossom.

Everyone hung up, leaving Bubbleisha staring at her phone. "Hello? Hello?" she tried.

A few moments later, a mob of Shoppies and Shopkins ran by her.

"Wait for me!" Bubbleisha called, and she ran after them.

They were off to meet the newest additions to Shopville!

CHAPTER 9

WHEN THE GROUP REACHED THE COOKING ACADEMY, they stared in awe at the building. It was made of piles of pots, pans, and kitchen utensils arranged in rows that stretched into long

hallways and high, shiny ceilings.

Donatina picked up a series of pots and tried to put each one on her head. "What are these strange things?" she asked. "Some sort of hat?"

"No, it's for cooking!" replied Lippy Lips, looking her friend up and down. "And it doesn't go with your shoes."

Donatina put the pots down and grabbed a whisk. "At least I know what these do!" She began to curl her hair with the kitchen utensil.

Lippy watched Donatina and just shook her head.

Meanwhile, Strawberry Tubs tried to get a taste of every edible item they passed. "Oh, this is so good!" she said, her mouth full. "And this. And this. And this!"

"Look! Over here!" called Bubbleisha. She had found an area where a big banner hung across the wall. It read:

CHEF CLUB!

"This must be the place!" said Miss Sprinkles.

"Or it could be a trap to make us think it's the Chef Club when it isn't," said Cheeky Chocolate, nudging Miss Sprinkles with her elbow.

"You think?" replied Miss Sprinkles, looking worried.

"No, I'm just messing with you," said Cheeky. She and Lippy began to laugh, causing Miss Sprinkles's sprinkles to turn bright red.

As the group continued to look around, a Shoppie and three Shopkins appeared and

stood beneath the banner.

The new Shoppie had long, mint-green hair that was held back by an ice-cream-cone headband. She blinked her mint-green eyes shyly and shuffled her ice-cream-cone shoes back and forth. It was clear she was nervous.

Next to her, there was a Shopkin that looked like a bunch of bananas, one that looked like a cup of noodles, and another that was shaped like a bowl.

"Um, hi, everybody," said the Shoppie in a quiet voice. "Have you come for the Chef Club?"

"We sure have!" replied the group as they crowded around the new Shoppie.

The Shoppie grabbed the noodle Shopkin and held her in front of her face like a mask. "I'm, um, Peppa-Mint," she continued.

"Welcome to Chef Club. This is, is . . . ," Peppa-Mint was very nervous speaking in front of such a big group.

The noodle Shopkin took over. "I am Nina Noodles." She pointed to the other Shopkins standing near Peppa-Mint. "That is Buncho Bananas. And she is Bessie Bowl."

Jessicake stepped forward with a smile. "I'm Jessicake. Nice to meet you all!"

Peppa-Mint peered out from behind Nina. "You have such pretty shoes!" she blurted out, admiring the cupcake heels that matched

Jessicake's frosting-blue hair.

"Thank you!" said Jessicake. She turned to Donatina. "And this is Donatina."

Peppa put Nina down. "You have a lovely name."

"Thank you!" said Donatina, smiling. "I've had it all my life!"

Bubbleisha stepped forward, fluffing up her bubbly pink curls. She was sure that Peppa would give her a nice compliment on them. "And I'm—"

But Miss Sprinkles bounced in front of Bubbleisha and leapt into Peppa-Mint's arms.

"Miss Sprinkles! And this is Lippy Lips!"

Peppa shook hands with Miss Sprinkles, then with Lippy. "Ah, what a lovely shade of pink," she said.

"So nice to meet you!" replied Lippy.

As Bubbleisha stood there with her hand out, Peppa-Mint was introduced to Cheeky Chocolate, Kooky Cookie, and the rest of the group.

"Wait," Bubbleisha said to herself. "Don't you want to meet me? I'm wearing a lovely shade of pink, too." Dumbfounded, she looked at her reflection in a nearby pot. "Don't I get a compliment?" But the rest of her friends had moved on.

"I'm glad to meet all of you," said Peppa-Mint when they had finished with introductions.

Bubbleisha sighed. She had missed her chance.

AFTER INTRODUCTIONS, APPLE BLOSSOM MADE an announcement. "We're joining Chef Club."

"It sounds great," said Jessicake. "But how do we get into Chef Club?"

Bessie Bowl cleared her throat. "To become a member, you will all be asked to cook four recipes, from getting the ingredients to cooking the dishes to the final tastings."

"I'm going to cook

up a storm, then eat it!" Strawberry Tubs declared. Her enthusiasm made her friends feel confident, too.

Before they got started, Peppa and Bessie began to point to Shoppies and Shopkins and group them together. "Donatina, Cheeky Chocolate, and Strawberry Tubs are in one group." Bessie looked around. "Jessicake, Apple Blossom, and . . . how about Miss Sprinkles? Which leaves you three as the final team." She pointed to Bubbleisha, Lippy Lips, and Kooky Cookie.

Buncho Bananas handed out recipes to each group. The first was for a dish called Spaghetti à la Boom.

The groups barely had time to look at the recipes when Bessie announced, "Let's get cooking!"

The friends wished one another good

luck and hurried off in their groups. Only Bubbleisha didn't rush off after everyone. She was still preoccupied with the compliments she hadn't received.

"I deserve a little 'atta girl,'" she said to herself. "A little 'Bubbleisha done good.' And I'm going to get it. How hard can cooking be?"

A FEW MOMENTS LATER, ALL THREE GROUPS were in the Small Mart. There was a mad rush as each Shoppie grabbed a shopping cart and the Shopkins on their team all piled inside.

Jessicake, Bubbleisha, and Donatina raced

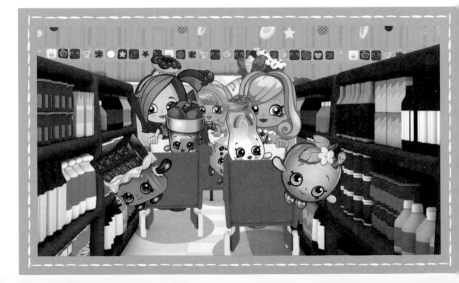

through the Small Mart aisles, pushing their carts at full speed.

"Last one to the ingredients is a squeaky shopping cart wheel!" cried Bubbleisha.

"It's not who gets there first, but who finds the stuff first!" replied Jessicake. "And we're great stuff finders, right, team?"

"We're the stuffiest finders around!" shouted Miss Sprinkles. She held on to the shopping cart handle as tightly as she could.

The Shoppies raced through the aisles with their carts. Bubbleisha was in the lead as she approached a turn. She was so excited that she was going to reach it first, that she accidentally cut off Donatina's cart when she went around the corner.

CRASH!

Donatina had to take the turn too tightly, and she knocked over a huge stack of cans. They went flying everywhere, bouncing and rolling down the aisle.

"Watch out!" cried Cheeky. "Incoming cans!"

Jessicake tried to steer her cart around the crazy cans, but it was too difficult to avoid them. The cans rolled into the cart, causing it to spin out of control and crash into a stack of cereal boxes.

"You okay?" called Cheeky.

Luckily, no one was hurt. Jessicake and her group were able to laugh off the minor setback and get back to their cart.

"The cereal boxes cushioned our wreck!" said Apple Blossom. "Who says breakfast isn't the most important meal of the day?"

Meanwhile, Bubbleisha was racing her cart by the pasta section. They needed some spaghetti for Spaghetti à la Boom, but Bubbleisha refused to slow down.

"Ready to grab spaghetti?" she called to her team. "Three . . . two . . . one . . . grab!"

Moving at full speed, Lippy latched her feet to the side of the cart and held Kooky's feet with her hands. As they raced by the spaghetti display, Kooky hung off the side of the cart and reached for a bag.

"Get it, Kooky! Get it!" cried Lippy.

Kooky managed to grab a bag of spaghetti and—

FWOMP!

Kooky hit the spaghetti bag at such a high speed that she was yanked from Lippy's hands. Now she and the bag of spaghetti were falling to the floor below.

"Koooooky!" Lippy shouted, terrified that

her friend would be hurt.

Luckily, Kooky was able to think fast. She took the chef hat from her head and held it above her like a parachute. It billowed out and gently took Kooky and the bag of spaghetti to the floor.

Just as she landed, Donatina scooped her and her bag of pasta up. She placed them both on the seat of her cart.

"Whew!" said Donatina. "You almost ended

up in aisle splat!"

"Thanks," replied Kooky.

Donatina hurried ahead and pushed her cart up next to Bubbleisha's.

"I believe you dropped this," she said, handing Kooky to Lippy.

"Kooky!" Lippy gave her friend a huge hug. "I thought you'd been pasta'd! Great job, Donatina!"

Bubbleisha heard Lippy's praise for Donatina and cringed. Where was her compliment?

After all, she had maintained her lead even after the crashes.

In a nearby aisle, Jessicake and her team were shopping for meatballs. They had come up with an excellent system for getting meatballs into their cart.

Apple Blossom sat on top of the meatball pile in the display counter and, one at a time, tossed meatballs up to Jessicake. Jessicake inspected each meatball and then dropped it down to Miss Sprinkles, who sat in the bottom of their cart.

"One meatball, if you please," said Apple as she tossed another meatball up to Jessicake.

"Thank you very much. And to you, Sprinkles," replied Jessicake, dropping the meatball down to Sprinkles.

After repeating this for several minutes, Sprinkles called up in a muffled voice. "A little help!" They had been working so well together that Jessicake and Apple hadn't realized that Sprinkles was now buried under a mound of meatballs!

In another aisle, Donatina and her team were working super speedily.

"Tomato sauce!" Cheeky read from the recipe card.

"Got it!" called Strawberry Tubs. She grabbed several cans as the team zoomed by a tomato sauce display, juggled them, then stacked them neatly in the cart. The team did the same with the onions.

But when they reached the Parmesan cheese, the container slipped out of Cheeky's hands, fell into the cart, and exploded, spraying Strawberry Tubs with powdered cheese. She began to sneeze uncontrollably. Each sneeze sent her flying around the cart like a pinball—but the team didn't let that stop them from moving ahead!

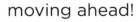

Despite their mishaps, all three teams soon made a final push to the doors of the Small Mart and raced cart to cart back to the Cooking Academy.

CHAPTER 5

WHEN THEY REACHED THE COOKING ACADEMY with their ingredients, all three teams dove right into the cooking portion of the competition. The main kitchen of the academy was abuzz with Shoppies and Shopkins running back and forth, measuring ingredients and throwing them into big pots bubbling on the stovetop.

"Whhaaahhaa!" cried Miss Sprinkles. She was dicing vegetables by riding on top of a food chopper like a pogo stick. When she was done, the veggies were arranged in the shape of a work of art!

"What a wonderful chopping job you did!" exclaimed Peppa-Mint when she passed by.

On the other side of the kitchen, Bubbleisha was calling out orders as fast as she could. Her team was frantically racing around, grabbing ingredients and dumping them into the pot.

"Two pinches, a tweak, and a pinkie of oregano!" called Bubbleisha.

CRASH!

In their effort to follow Bubbleisha's directions, Lippy and Kooky ran right into each other!

"Two what of what's with a pinkie what?" asked Lippy when she had recovered her footing. Kooky just scratched her head and shrugged.

As Peppa-Mint passed by, she took the teaspoon and measured out the perfect amount of oregano, then dumped it in the pot.

"Thanks!" said Lippy.

"Don't mention it," replied Peppa-Mint. "You're doing a great job."

Bubbleisha frowned. She was the head of this team. Why wasn't she the one being complimented? "I did a great job, too," she said under her breath.

Nearby, Donatina and Cheeky were trying

to measure out their spaghetti.

Cheeky examined the recipe. "It says exactly one hundred strands," she said.

Donatina grabbed a handful of spaghetti and began counting. "One piece of spaghetti. Two pieces of spaghetti. Three pieces of spaghetti . . ."

At this rate, measuring the spaghetti would take forever! Thankfully, Peppa-Mint came by and grabbed a handful of spaghetti. "I think that's one hundred."

"Really?" Donatina started counting Peppa-

Mint's pile. "One piece of spaghetti . . ."

"Here. Let me!" said Cheeky. She grabbed Peppa-Mint's handful of spaghetti and tossed it into the pot of boiling water. Then she turned to Peppa-Mint and said quietly, "Thanks. We might have been here all month!"

"She's doing a good job, though!" replied Peppa-Mint.

Once each team had their spaghetti cooking, they prepared to move on to the next step of the recipe. It was the most important—and the most dangerous.

"EVERYONE? EVERYONE?" PEPPA—MINT TRIED to get the group's attention, but no one could hear her over the bustling and bubbling of the kitchen.

"LISTEN UP!" yelled Buncho Bananas, startling everyone—including Peppa-Mint! Scared stiff as a board, she fell over in surprise, but quickly stood back up again. She grabbed Nina and held her in front of her face.

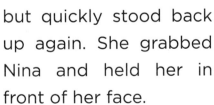

"All right, everyone," Bessie began. "It's time

to put the popcorn in. Carefully lower the kernels into your heated sauce. Again, carefully, or you might get a big boom-boom!"

Bubbleisha measured out her kernels and carefully poured them into her team's sauce. "Kernels in the hole!" she called out as a warning. Everyone ducked down, bracing for an explosion. But nothing happened. "We did it!" exclaimed Bubbleisha.

As Donatina prepared to pour her kernels in, Cheeky Chocolate and Strawberry Tubs cheered her on. "You can do it, Donatina!"

Donatina covered her eyes with one hand and poured the kernels into their sauce with the other. She uncovered her eyes.

"Did it work?" she asked, only to discover that she had missed the pot completely and poured the kernels into a measuring cup that had been resting right next to the pot. "Oops."

She poured the measuring cup full of kernels into the pot with no explosions!

Finally, Jessicake picked up her cup full of kernels. "I hope I do this okay," she said nervously.

"Don't worry! We'll help!" said Apple Blossom and Miss Sprinkles. They rushed over to Jessicake and accidentally bumped into her arm, causing her to drop the whole cup of kernels into the pot. *Plop!*

The teammates watched the pot, horrified, but nothing happened. Just when they breathed a sigh of relief—

KABLAM! The pot exploded, splattering sauce everywhere. Jessicake and her team were completely covered, and every other Shoppie and Shopkin in the room had splatters on them.

"This is so clashing with my shoes," said Lippy.

The room was quiet for a moment—then everyone started laughing.

"I like it when the meatballs blow up," whispered Buncho Bananas.

Peppa-Mint tasted some sauce that had landed on her cheek. "You, um," she began. "Um . . ."

"What she's trying to say," Bessie jumped in, "is that you all passed—" The group cheered. "—but this one really put the *boom* in Spaghetti à la Boom! Great job!"

Covered in sauce, Jessicake and her team began dancing and cheering in celebration. The other teams came over to congratulate them, but Bubbleisha stood aside, upset that her team's recipe wasn't getting special attention.

"We're going to do better next time, right, girls?" she said to Kooky and Lippy when they had gathered together again.

Kooky shrugged.

"We all passed," said Lippy.

Bubbleisha pursed her lips. "I think we can pass better," she replied. "Don't we deserve a little recognition, too?"

Lippy and Kooky didn't understand what she meant, but Bubbleisha was determined to stand out in the next test.

ONCE THE KITCHEN HAD BEEN CLEANED UP, Bessie announced the next test.

"Your challenge is to make a Chili-Chocolate Licorice Tower. The higher and chillier, the better! Go cook!"

Donatina and her team headed to Petkins Park to get the best chili for their recipe. In a small, grassy area of the park, Donatina pushed a large plow.

"I. Think. I'm. Doing. Something. Wrong," gasped Donatina.

"Nope, you're doing great!" said Cheeky.

Strawberry Tubs followed behind the plow and planted seeds in each row that Donatina created.

"We're going to grow an Ultimillivanilli Chili with these Super-Gro seeds!" said Cheeky.

Donatina gave the plow an extra-hard push and slipped, falling face-first into the mud.

"Way to put your face into it, Donatina!" cheered Strawberry Tubs.

Meanwhile, Jessicake and her team were at the Sweets Shop admiring a giant spool of licorice that hung from the ceiling. It was exactly what they needed for their recipe. There was just one problem.

"How do we get up there?" asked Jessicake.

The team had an idea. Miss Sprinkles did a little stretch, then Jessicake picked her up and tossed her toward the licorice spool.

"Wahoooo!" cried Miss Sprinkles as she

sailed through the air and grabbed on to the end of the licorice.

"You did it!" cheered Jessicake and Apple Blossom from below.

The group had been hoping that Miss Sprinkles's weight would be enough to pull down the licorice. But she wasn't moving.

Apple Blossom volunteered to help, so Jessicake launched her toward the spool next.

Apple Blossom flew toward Sprinkles and grabbed hold of her feet. Even with the extra weight, the licorice still wouldn't move, so Apple Blossom began to wiggle and shake. Finally, the licorice started to unspool.

It began to move faster and faster. Soon, it was spinning out of control.

"Whaaaaaa!" cried Sprinkles and Apple Blossom as they fell to the floor and landed on Jessicake. The team was quickly covered under a mountain of licorice.

"I think something's stuck in my hair . . . ," said Jessicake from beneath the licorice pile.

This was not going exactly as they had planned.

In an office at the back of the Small Mart, Bubbleisha, Lippy Lips, and Kooky Cookie crept around quietly.

"There's a super-secret-double-hidden freezer back here that has what we're looking for," said Bubbleisha. She added quietly to herself, "Then we'll see who gets told how great and wonderful they are."

At the back of the office, the team found a giant steel freezer that was secured with tons of locks. Bubbleisha took out a ring of keys and began unlocking them one by one.

"Okay, glasses on!" Bubbleisha announced. "What's inside is nuclear." Bubbleisha handed Kooky the tongs, then placed her on top of the freezer. "Just get *one*. Anything more may cause a rift in the space-time continuum."

Kooky carefully used the tongs to push open the top of the freezer, releasing a bright, frosty light. She reached in and grabbed something with the tongs, then raised it out for her friends to see. It was a small, neon-red chili pepper that glowed with heat.

"Behold the radioactive Lava-Lava Chili Pepper!" said Bubbleisha. "It's said to be hotter than the center of the sun!" She held out the special container and Kooky dropped the pepper inside. "At last, my ticket to getting noticed," Bubbleisha said to herself as she snapped the container shut.

BACK AT THE COOKING ACADEMY, LIPPY AND

Kooky were stirring a big pot of melted chocolate while Bubbleisha sat nearby, petting the container that held the Lava-Lava Chili.

"You shall be my *seeeee*cret weapon," she purred.

"Bubbleisha's losing it," Lippy said to Kooky. "I hope she knows what she's doing."

Nearby, Jessicake's team was braiding a

giant pile of licorice to make a licorice pyramid.

SQUEAK! SQUEAK! SQUEAK!

Everyone looked up to see Donatina's team pushing a wagon into the kitchen. It held a giant green chili pepper.

"Behold Pepperzilla!" announced Cheeky.

Bubbleisha rushed over to Peppa-Mint. "That's cheating!" she cried.

Peppa-Mint con-sulted with Nina, Buncho Bananas, and Bessie. After a moment, Bessie declared, "Judges ruling: It's a chili, so it is not cheating. All is fair in love and cooking."

Stunned, Bubbleisha grasped her special container. "Then we will fight fire with fire,

won't we, little pepper?" She turned to Lippy and Kooky. "Is the chocolate sauce ready?"

Lippy and Kooky nodded.

"Glasses on!" ordered Bubbleisha. Using tongs, she pulled the Lava-Lava Chili from its container and brought it to the pot of chocolate sauce.

Kooky tugged on Bubbleisha's arm. "Too much!" she warned.

"No," replied Bubbleisha. "I want to use the whole thing. Too much is never enough!" And she dropped the whole pepper into the sauce.

Bubbleisha watched with delight as the chocolate sauce began to boil and bubble. Then her eyes widened in fear.

"Hit the floor!" she cried. She grabbed her friends and dove to the floor just as—*KA-BOOM!* The sauce erupted, spraying chocolate all over Bubbleisha and her team.

"Mmmm," said Kooky as she licked chocolate off of Lippy.

Just then, the judges announced that it was time to taste all the recipes. Donatina's team had put a small bunch of licorice on top of their giant pepper and slathered it with chocolate sauce. Jessicake's team had created a chocolate-covered-licorice version of the Golden Gate Bridge. Bubbleisha's team wore most of their recipe but had managed to drip some chocolate sauce on a messy pile of licorice.

When Peppa-Mint and her Shopkins had tasted each one, Bessie stepped forward. "You've all passed."

The group cheered, but Bubbleisha wasn't

satisfied. "Was one, you know, wonderful? Great?"

"Yes," said Bessie, sounding distracted. "Cheeky's group was wonderfully tall. And Jessicake's team was artistically great."

"And your group was . . . ," Peppa-Mint began. But before she could finish, Nina Noodles came running through the kitchen, her tongue the color of the Lava-Lava Chili.

"Water-water-water!" she cried. Apple Blossom handed Nina glass after glass of water, and Nina chugged each one until her mouth had finally cooled.

"Okay, show's over," Bessie announced. "The next recipe is . . ." She looked to Peppa-Mint.

"Guum Guum Fruit Stuffed with Guum Guum Fruit?" finished Peppa-Mint.

"Go, everyone!" said Nina.

The teams rushed off with their new recipe cards, leaving only Bubbleisha behind.

"What about my compliment?" she whispered. "Grr!" She ran after her team, determined to make the best Guum Guum Fruit recipe anyone had ever tasted.

ALL THREE TEAMS GATHERED IN PETKINS PARK

near a big, bushy tree with huge, multi-colored fruit hanging from its branches. On its trunk was the grumpy face of an old man.

"Remember," said Peppa-Mint, "Guum Guum trees are very moody and don't like to have their fruit touched by anyone. So good luck and, uh, be careful!"

Donatina and her team approached the

tree first. They carried trays full of cakes, cup-
cakes, cookies, and brownies.

"You want my fruit, don't ya?" said the tree.
"Well, you can't have any, so there."

"Oh, but we want to trade," said Donatina
sweetly.

"We have all sorts of yummy-for-your-
tummy goodies," said Strawberry Tubs.

The tree was skeptical, but he allowed
Donatina to approach and dump a whole plate
of cookies into his mouth.

"That's not bad," he said, licking his lips.

"Maybe I'll try a little more."

Donatina and her team poured tray after tray of sweets into the tree's mouth. He kept wanting more until—

"Oooh, I don't feel so good," said the tree. He let out a loud burp, and Guum Guum Fruit rained down on Donatina's team. After another small burp, the tree announced, "I feel much better now." Donatina, Strawberry Tubs, and Cheeky Chocolate happily grabbed the fallen fruit and went to get started on their recipe.

Rather than giving him more sweets, Jessicake and her team decided to give the tree a makeover. Apple Blossom tied a big bow in his branches, while Sprinkles used a huge mascara brush on his lashes. Jessicake sat on the ground and gave each branch a manicure.

"The polish is going to totally highlight your bark," said Jessicake.

"I'm going to be a new tree!" exclaimed the Guum Guum. He was so happy with his makeover that he gladly allowed Jessicake and her team to take some of his fruit.

"Okay, our turn," said Bubbleisha to her team. "I've got just the plan."

A few moments later, Bubbleisha snuck up behind the tree and blew a huge, blaring airhorn. The tree was so shocked, he screamed and dropped all his fruit. Bubbleisha, Lippy, and Kooky grabbed as much fruit as they could carry and ran.

"I'll teach you to scare a poor defenseless tree!" the Guum Guum called after them. Then

he hurled a piece of fruit at Bubbleisha's head. It hit her and splattered gooey juice all over her.

"Ha! More fruit for me," Bubbleisha says, not wanting Guum Guum to know he got to her. But as she walked away, she rubbed her head- where the fruit had hit her. "Ow!"

A little while later, Peppa-Mint and the Chef Club members walked around the kitchen tasting each team's Guum Guum Fruit Stuffed with Guum Guum Fruit.

"It's all quite wonderful," said Peppa-Mint. "You all passed. Just one last recipe, and then I bet you all make it into Chef Club!"

Everyone cheered, but Bubbleisha was lost in thought. "There's got to be something I can do to get noticed around here . . ."

CHAPTER 10

THAT AFTERNOON, EACH TEAM EAGERLY READ their last recipe card for Upside-Down Hula-Hoop Soup—with real Hula-Hoops.

Bubbleisha clutched the recipe to her chest and looked around the room suspiciously. "We need an edge," she said to Kooky and Lippy.

"No way," said Lippy. "I get paper cuts too easily."

"No, an edge to do better than the others," said Bubbleisha impatiently.

"Like cheating?" Lippy looked uncomfortable with this suggestion.

"No, no. Sort of. But not," said Bubbleisha.

"Just something to make sure we do a better job than the others."

Kooky looked at her in confusion. "But we want everyone to get into Chef Club, right?"

"Yes," said Bubbleisha. "I just want us to get in ahead of everyone so people notice and say nice things about me—er, us. Don't worry," she added. "I just need you two to hold the rope."

Bubbleisha had Lippy and Kooky lower her from the ceiling. She hovered over the other teams and skillfully switched out each of their recipe cards with another one.

"There," said Bubbleisha when Lippy and Kooky had pulled her safely back up to the rafters. "Now we have the right recipe and they don't. It's dinner take all!"

That evening, all three groups were franti-

cally cooking—and hula-hooping. Jessicake and Donatina's teams were stirring normal-size pots, but Bubbleisha was cooking her team's soup in a giant pot that was over twenty feet high.

"If only they knew their recipes had the wrong amounts," she said to herself.

Peppa-Mint and the Chef Club members walked from team to team to check everyone's progress.

As they passed Jessicake's team, Bessie told them their recipe needed more salt. "I calculate one single grain more."

They soon reached Bubbleisha's team and looked up at the giant pot.

"I see you're making extra for everyone?" said Peppa-Mint.

"Nope, it's what the recipe says." Bubbleisha held out the recipe card. "See?"

The Chef Club members all crowded around Peppa-Mint to look at the recipe.

"Oh, dear," said Peppa-Mint. "The amounts aren't right at all!"

Bubbleisha's eyes nearly bulged out of her head. "But . . . how?"

Nearby, Kooky began to whistle, trying to

look innocent—but it was clear that she had switched the recipe.

Bubbleisha began to seethe. Her face grew redder and redder as she grew angrier and angrier. She grabbed a handful of

ingredients and hurled them into Jessicake's pot.

The splash splattered Apple Blossom. She thought Bubbleisha was joking around. "Two can play that game!" Apple Blossom said, grabbing more ingredients and throwing them at Bubbleisha's pot, laughing. She missed and hit Donatina instead.

Donatina giggled and joined in, tossing ingredients at Bubbleisha.

"Hey!" yelled Bubbleisha. "You almost got it in my soup!"

"Food fight!" shouted Lippy.

Suddenly, food was flying everywhere. The girls were all laughing and squealing—except Bubbleisha. She was serious—and seriously angry. As she hurled food at her friends with both hands, she accidentally hit the knob under her giant pot's burner. The temperature went from **WARM** to **HOT** to **VOLCANO**.

Soon, the pot was boiling so violently it looked like it was going to explode!

WITH FOOD FLYING EVERYWHERE, KOOKY WAS

the only one who noticed the giant pot about to erupt. She tried to get Bubbleisha's attention, but Bubbleisha was too busy throwing food.

In a panic, Kooky rushed over to the stove-top and tried to twist the knob back down. It was stuck. She grabbed a fork and tried to use it as a lever to move the knob. The knob still wouldn't budge. The fork bent back and flung Kooky through the air. She landed safely on a loaf of bread and looked up in time to see a fountain of soup explode from the pot and pour over the side like a giant soup waterfall.

The soup quickly flooded the kitchen and swept Kooky, still on the loaf of bread, out into the street!

The food fight came to an abrupt stop as everyone realized what had just happened.

"Oh, no! Kooky!" cried Apple Blossom. "We have to help her!" Everyone except Bubbleisha rushed out of the kitchen and after Kooky.

Left alone with the gushing pot of soup, Bubbleisha was still angry. "Come on! Let's hear those compliments!" She added a mocking tone to her voice. "Great mess, Bubbleisha! Wonderful way you blew up the soup and sent Kooky to her certain doom, Bubbleisha."

Bubbleisha stopped as she realized what she had just said. "Kooky! Oh, no! What did I do?" Determined, she looked around the kitchen. She grabbed a bunch of spoons and a stack of Hula-Hoops. "I'll fix it!"

CHAPTER 12

AS THE STREETS OF SHOPVILLE FLOODED WITH soup, Kooky rode her loaf of bread like a life raft while she was tossed and turned in every direction.

Meanwhile, the other Shoppies and Shopkins were racing down a side street in an effort to get in front of the soup flood.

"Faster!" cried Cheeky. "We have to get ahead before Kooky smashes or goes under!"

Apple Blossom, Lippy, Cheeky, and Jessicake raced ahead and jumped on a fence that lined the flooded street. Jessicake dug her fingers into her hair and

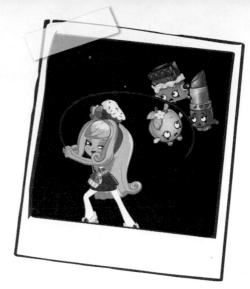

pulled out a piece of licorice.

"Grab hold!" she told the Shopkins. When they did, she began to spin the licorice around her head like a lasso.

"This is so not fun," said Lippy, who was beginning to turn green. "Green is not my color."

Jessicake spotted Kooky about to speed by on her loaf of bread and aimed the spinning licorice at her. Apple, Cheeky, and Lippy were able to grab on to the loaf. But when Jessicake tried to yank everyone to safety, she lost her grip on the licorice.

Now Kooky, Apple, Cheeky, and Lippy were

all stranded on the loaf of bread! The rest of the Shoppies and Shopkins looked on in desperation.

"What do we do now?" asked Miss Sprinkles.

"Get some crackers?" suggested Donatina. "Soup always goes better with crackers."

"We better do it fast!" cried Strawberry Tubs. "Look!" She pointed to a wall up ahead. The loaf of bread was heading right toward it!

"Did someone say fast?" came a voice from the soup. It was Bubbleisha! She was riding through the flood in a big soup dish. "Jump in!"

The Shopkins on shore jumped into the dish as Bubbleisha sped by. "Grab a spoon and paddle like Kooky's life depends on it," ordered Bubbleisha, "because it does!"

"Stroke! Stroke! Stroke! Stroke!" Nina shouted from the back of the dish.

Together, they moved the dish ahead. They were almost to Kooky's loaf raft, and the wall was getting closer and closer.

"Now or never ever!" shouted Bubbleisha. "Jump for it!"

The Shopkins on the loaf of bread leapt toward the dish. Lippy, Apple, and Cheeky made it!

But Kooky wasn't able to jump far enough. She fell toward the soup and—

WHOOSH!

Bubbleisha caught her just in time!

"Can't let anything happen to my teammate!" said Bubbleisha.

Kooky looked at Bubbleisha gratefully and breathed a sigh of relief. Then—

Smoosh! The loaf of bread smashed against the wall and sank into the swirling soup.

The dish was next!

"PADDLE THE OTHER WAY IN REVERSE!" CRIED

Bubbleisha as the dish sped toward the wall.

The Shopkins paddled their spoons furiously in the opposite direction. They managed to

stop the dish from hitting the wall, but they weren't able to move away from it. They struggled to hold their position inches away from the wall.

"What now?" cried

Strawberry Tubs, straining to keep her spoon moving. "My paddling's pooping out!"

Just then, they heard a voice from above. "Anything we can do to help?"

It was Jessicake! She and Peppa-Mint were standing on top of the wall.

Bubbleisha smiled with relief. "Oh, thank you, thank you, thank you for lending a hand!"

"Besties help besties!" replied Jessicake.

Bubbleisha pulled the Hula-Hoops from her waist and tossed them up to the other Shoppies, revealing that the hoops were all connected. The Shoppies on the wall grabbed one end while Bubbleisha hung on to the other.

"Hold tight and one, two, three, pull!" shouted Jessicake.

"Hang on!" cried Bubbleisha. The Shopkins in the dish clung to her, and they were all yanked upward by the chain of Hula-Hoops.

"Ahhhh!" the friends cried as they flew through the air. They landed safely on top of the wall just in time to see the dish crash into it and sink.

The Shoppies and Shopkins began to whoop and cheer. They piled into a giant group hug that almost sent them falling off the wall. Luckily, they steadied themselves in time.

Everyone was safe!

CHAPTER 14

EXHAUSTED AND COVERED IN SOUP, THE FRIENDS made their way back to the Cooking Academy and looked around in defeat. The place was even more of a mess than they were.

"What do we do now?" asked Apple Blossom. "All our soups are souped."

"I guess . . . no Chef Club for us," replied Cheeky Chocolate.

The teams watched, perplexed, as Peppa-Mint and the Chef Club members went around the kitchen tasting the splattered remains of the final Upside-Down Hula-Hoop Soup.

"What's she doing?" whispered Miss Sprinkles.

"Having lunch?" suggested Donatina.

They grew anxious as they realized the Chef Club members were judging the splotches of soup.

"But how can anyone tell whose recipe is whose?" asked Strawberry Tubs. "They're all mixed up."

Finally, Peppa-Mint, Nina Noodles, Buncho Bananas, and Bessie Bowl turned to the group and smiled.

"And it's all so good, you all pass," declared Peppa-Mint. "Congratulations! You are all official members of the Chef Club."

The rest of the Shoppies and Shopkins stood in shock for a moment. Then they began cheering, jumping up and down, and hugging each other.

"And, um, all thanks to Bubbleisha for saving the day and being very brave," added Peppa-Mint.

Everyone began to praise Bubbleisha.

"You're so great!"

"You're so wonderful!"

"You're so brave!"

A huge smile spread across Bubbleisha's face as she took in the com-pliments. But then her smile fell.

"I don't deserve your compliments," she said. "Even though I want-ed them more than anything in the world. I wanted them too much."

"But you do deserve them!" said Jessicake. "You saved Kooky!"

Bubbleisha shook her head. "But I put her in danger, all because I wanted just one, silly little compliment."

"But you get compliments all the time!" insisted Apple Blossom. "Why, just the other day . . . " She thought for a moment. "Hmm."

"Didn't she get a compliment for . . . ," began Cheeky, but she didn't come up with anything.

"Wow," said Lippy. "Maybe we have been a little short in the compliment department. We're sorry."

"You're the best shopper!" said Apple Blossom.

"You're brave!" said Lippy.

"You always have good advice!" added Jessicake.

The compliments came faster and faster until Bubbleisha began to blush. She burst out laughing. "Okay, okay! Thanks for the compliments!" Then she looked at Kooky. "You forgive me?"

"Of course, 'cause you're the greatest at getting me into trouble," said Kooky. "And getting me out of it." She gave Bubbleisha a big hug.

"So," began Cheeky, "now that that's settled and we're in, when do we get to meet all the other Chef Club members?"

Peppa-Mint blushed with embarrassment. "Well, um," she began, "there are no other members because, you see, we kind of . . ."

"Invented Chef Club," finished Bessie.

Everyone exchanged confused, and slightly angry, looks.

Peppa-Mint turned an even deeper shade of red. "We're new here," she explained, "and it  was just a way to make friends. And you girls are such good friends, so nice, so caring . . ."

Now everyone else began to blush as well.

"We hope," Peppa-Mint continued, "you'll all be our friends, too?" She, Buncho Bananas, Nina, and Bessie looked at the rest of the group, eagerly awaiting their response.

The group looked at one another. Then Miss Sprinkles spoke for them all. "Well, yay! Who doesn't want more friends?"

"And since we all know how to cook now, we can make the biggest feast ever!" cheered Apple Blossom. "Chef Club rules!"

Together, the Shoppies and Shopkins cleaned the Cooking Academy and transformed it into the best party space anyone had ever seen. There were tables full of colorful decorations. There was great music. And, of course, there was a ton of delicious food—including Spaghetti à la Boom, a Chili-Chocolate Licorice Tower, Guum Guum Fruit Stuffed with Guum Guum Fruit, and Upside-Down Hula-Hoop Soup.

Most important of all, there were friends, old and new—and they were all part of the best Chef Club ever!